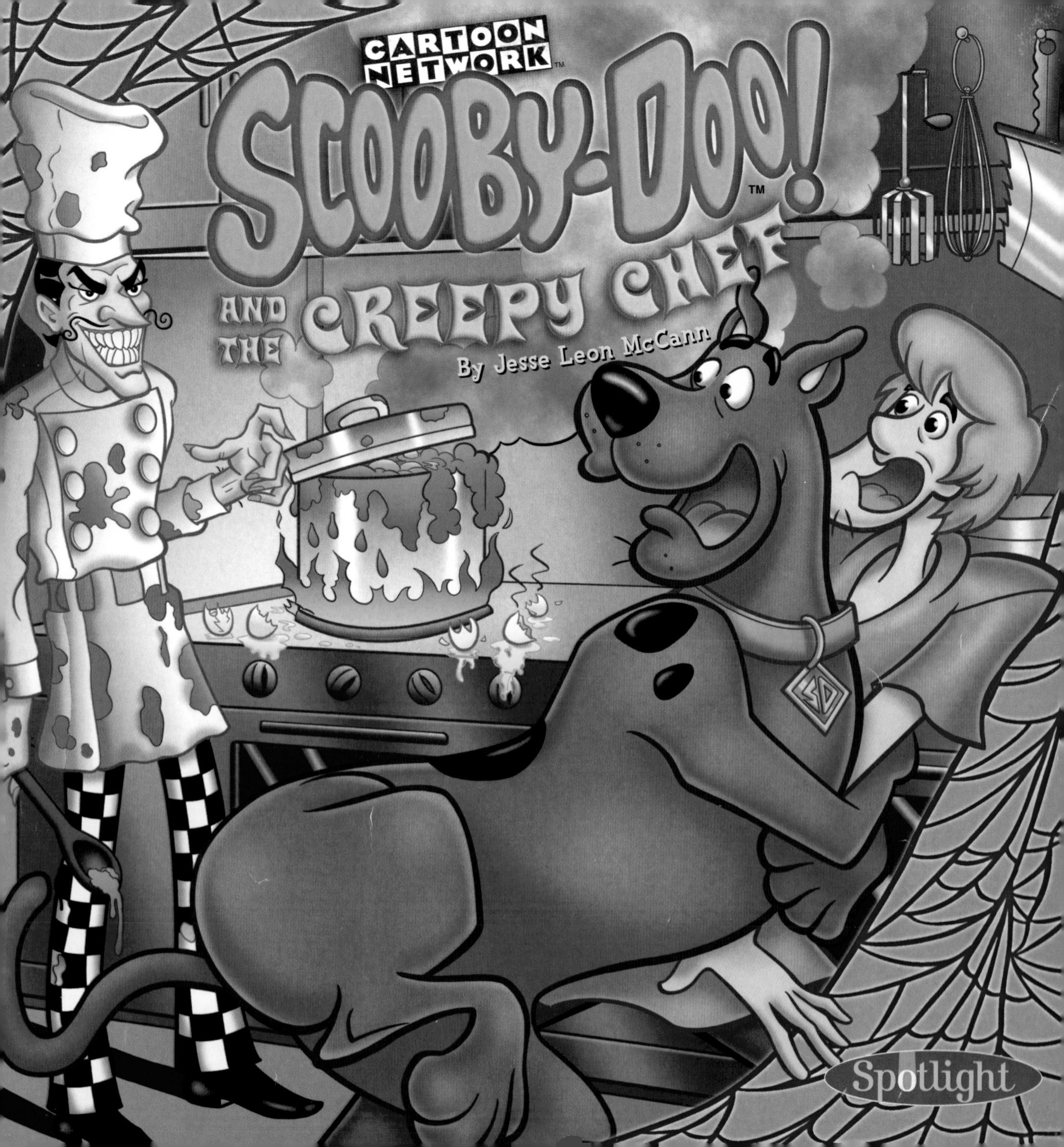
CARTOON NETWORK™
SCOOBY-DOO!™
AND THE CREEPY CHEF
By Jesse Leon McCann
Spotlight

visit us at www.abdopublishing.com

Reinforced library bound edition published in 2010 by Spotlight, a division of the ABDO Group, 8000 West 78th Street, Edina, Minnesota 55439. Spotlight produces high-quality reinforced library bound editions for schools and libraries. Published by agreement with Warner Bros.—A Time Warner Company. The stories, characters, and incidents mentioned are entirely fictional. All rights reserved. Used under authorization.

Printed in the United States of America, Melrose Park, Illinois.
092009
012010

 PRINTED ON RECYCLED PAPER

Special thanks to Duendes del Sur for cover and interior illustrations.

Library of Congress Cataloging-in-Publication Data

McCann, Jesse Leon.
  Scooby-Doo and the creepy chef / by Jesse Leon McCann ; [cover and interior illustrations, Dan Davis]. --
Reinforced library bound ed.
     p. cm.
  ISBN 978-1-59961-676-6
  I. Davis, Dan W. II. Scooby-Doo (Television program) III. Title.
  PZ7.M47835Sbi 2010
  [Fic]--dc22
                                                                          2009031238

All Spotlight books are reinforced library binding
and manufactured in the United States of America.

Scooby-Doo and his pals from Mystery, Inc. were invited to a local cooking school to be contest judges.

"Roh boy, roh boy," Scooby licked his lips hungrily.

"Man, you said it, Scoob," Shaggy smiled. "Like, what could be better than free food and lots of it?"

COOLSVILLE
CULINARY
INSTITUTE

ANNUAL COOKING
CONTEST TODAY!

"Be serious, boys," Velma said. "This contest is very important to the students. The winner gets a $500 cash prize."

As they entered the school, they were met by Mr. Kettle, the organizer of the cooking competition. He had a mystery brewing for Scooby and the gang.

4

Early that morning, when the students assembled, they were attacked by a creepy chef. Some of the students were so scared, they didn't come back.

5

Shaggy and Scooby didn't like the idea of a haunted school, but by the time they reached the main kitchen they had forgotten all about that. The sight of all the items used to make yummy meals made their tummies growl.

"Ready, set, go!" Velma said, and the cooking contest began.

But as soon as the competition started, it was interrupted. The creepy chef appeared out of nowhere and chanted in an eerie voice

"Ha, ha, ha, and ho, ho, ho! Isn't it time that everyone ate?

No need to cook a meal. Have spaghetti from my plate."

Ordinarily, Shaggy and Scooby would love some spaghetti, but not this kind.

"Zoinks!" Shaggy cried. "Those aren't noodles, they're worms."

"Rurms?" Scooby-Doo gulped. "Roh, yuck!"

"We need to find this creepy chef," Fred explained. "Shaggy, you and Scooby check the storage areas. The girls and I will go back to the classroom."

"Don't eat any food," Velma said. "It belongs to the school."
"Raw, shucks," Scooby was very disappointed. So was Shaggy.

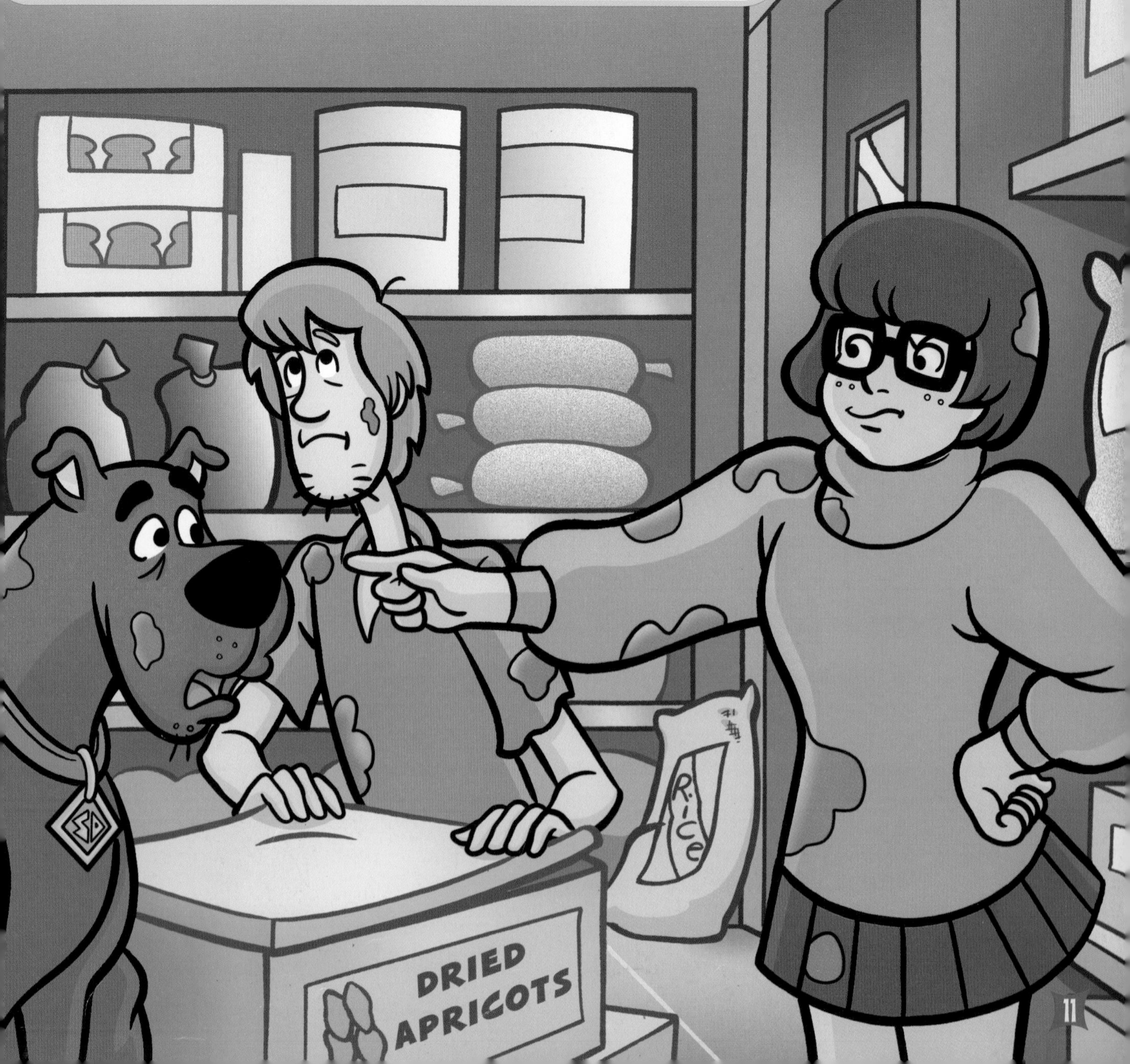
RICE
DRIED APRICOTS

"Like, goodies, goodies everywhere, and not a drop to eat," Shaggy complained. "The school wouldn't mind if we had a tiny sniff of this chocolate pudding, would they?"

"Ruh-uh," Scooby agreed.

Scooby and Shaggy didn't get what they hoped for when they opened the container. What they got were bugs, and lots of them.

"Roh noooo!" Scooby cried. "Run, Raggy, run!"

"Like, I'm with you, old pal," agreed Shaggy.

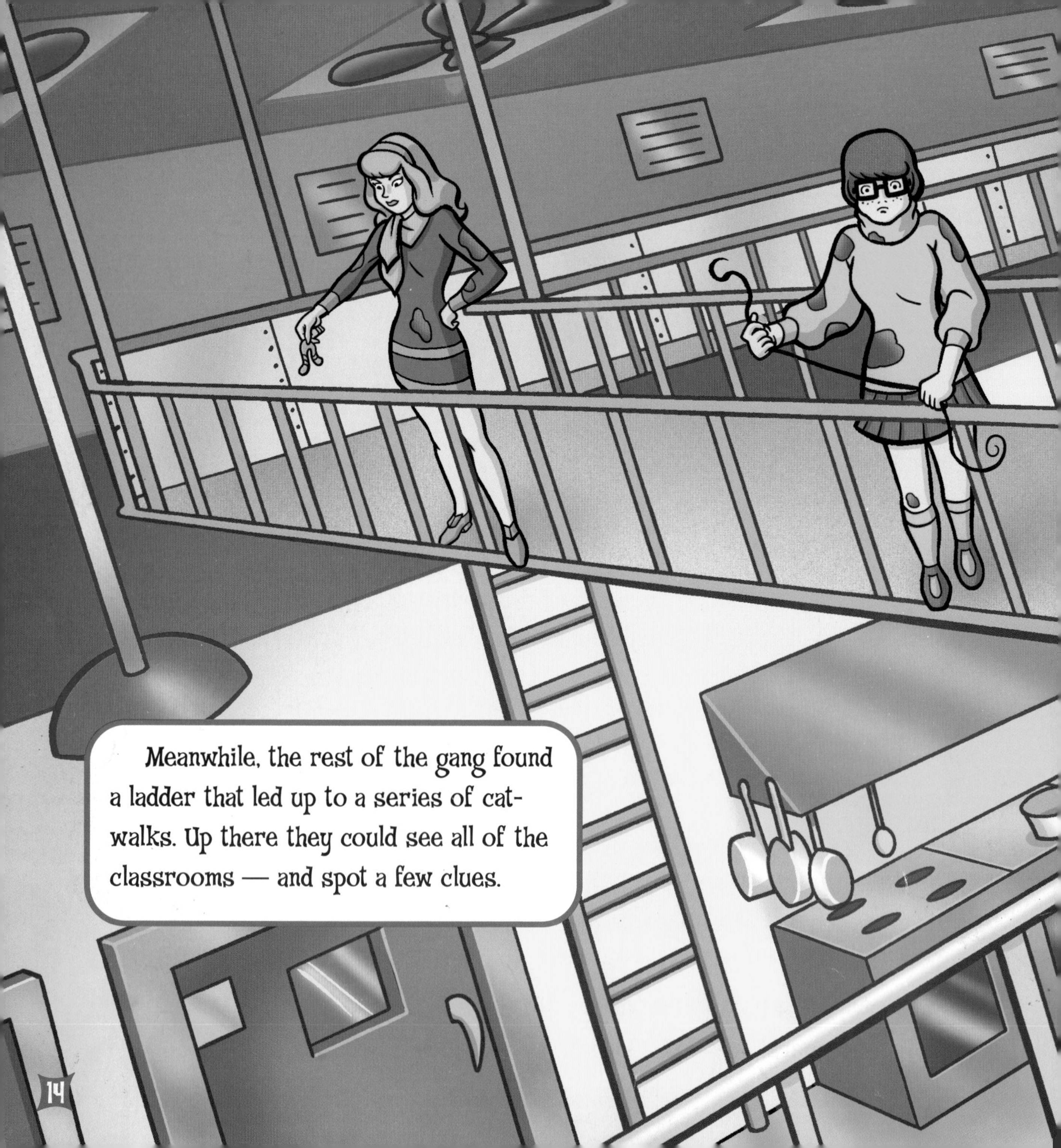

Meanwhile, the rest of the gang found a ladder that led up to a series of cat-walks. Up there they could see all of the classrooms — and spot a few clues.

"Look at this thin wire," Velma remarked. "What could it be for?"

"Eww, jeepers! A worm!" Daphne said. "What is it doing up here?"

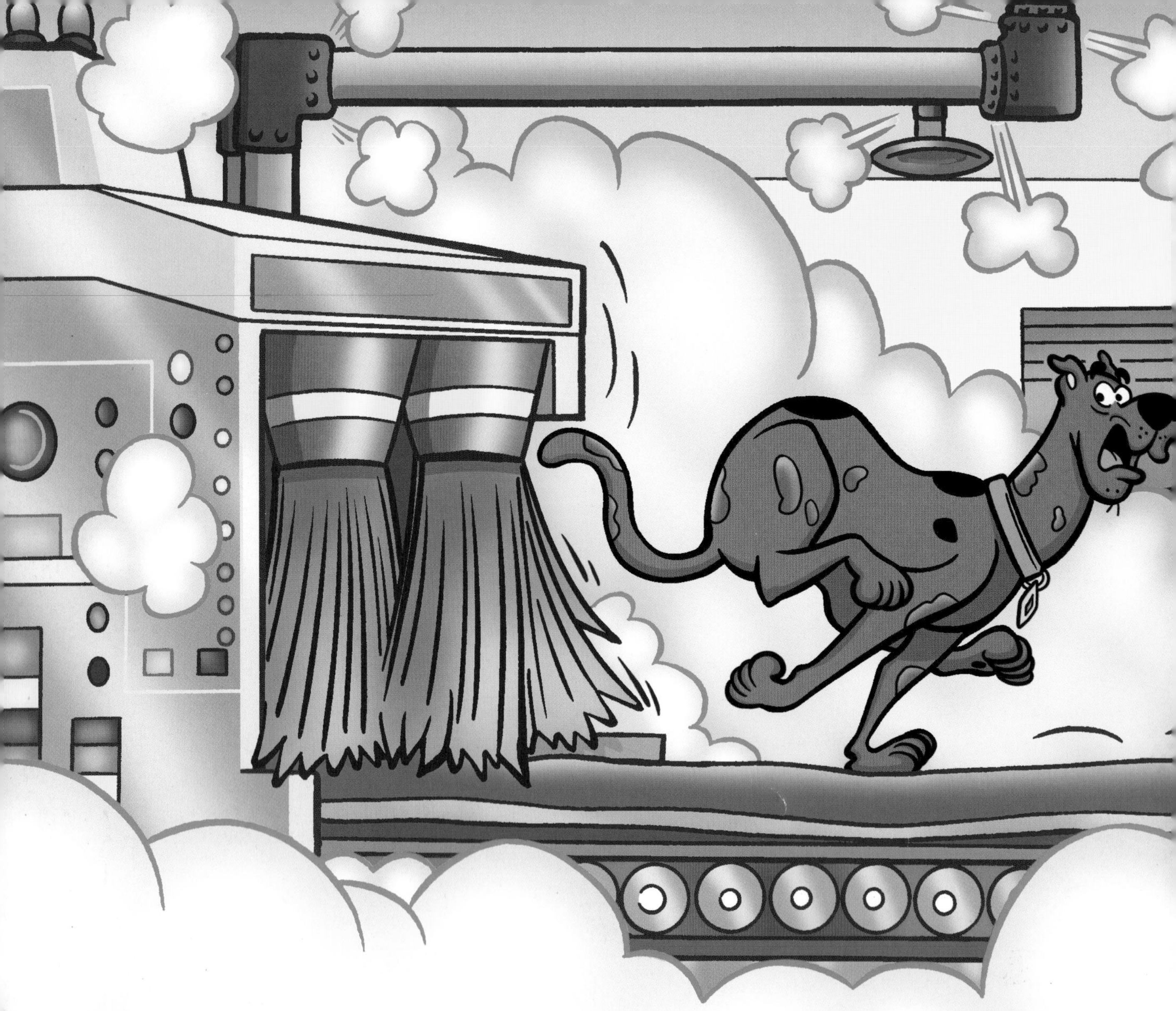

Scooby and Shaggy were in trouble! Scalding hot, whirling trouble.
"Like, Scoob, how do we stop this crazy thing?" Shaggy hollered.
"I ron't know! I ron't know!" Scooby cried. "Roh-ooh-ooh!"

They ran, but didn't go anywhere. They hadn't noticed that the creepy chef had turned up the conveyor belt to its fastest setting.

Low | Medium | High

Finally free from the dishwasher, Shaggy and Scooby ran into a freezer. Luckily, the creepy chef didn't want to follow, and the rest of the gang was already inside. Fred had thought of a plan to catch the creepy chef.

18

"All we need is Shaggy and Scooby to get his attention," Fred said. "Zoinks!" Shaggy exclaimed. "I knew you would say that."

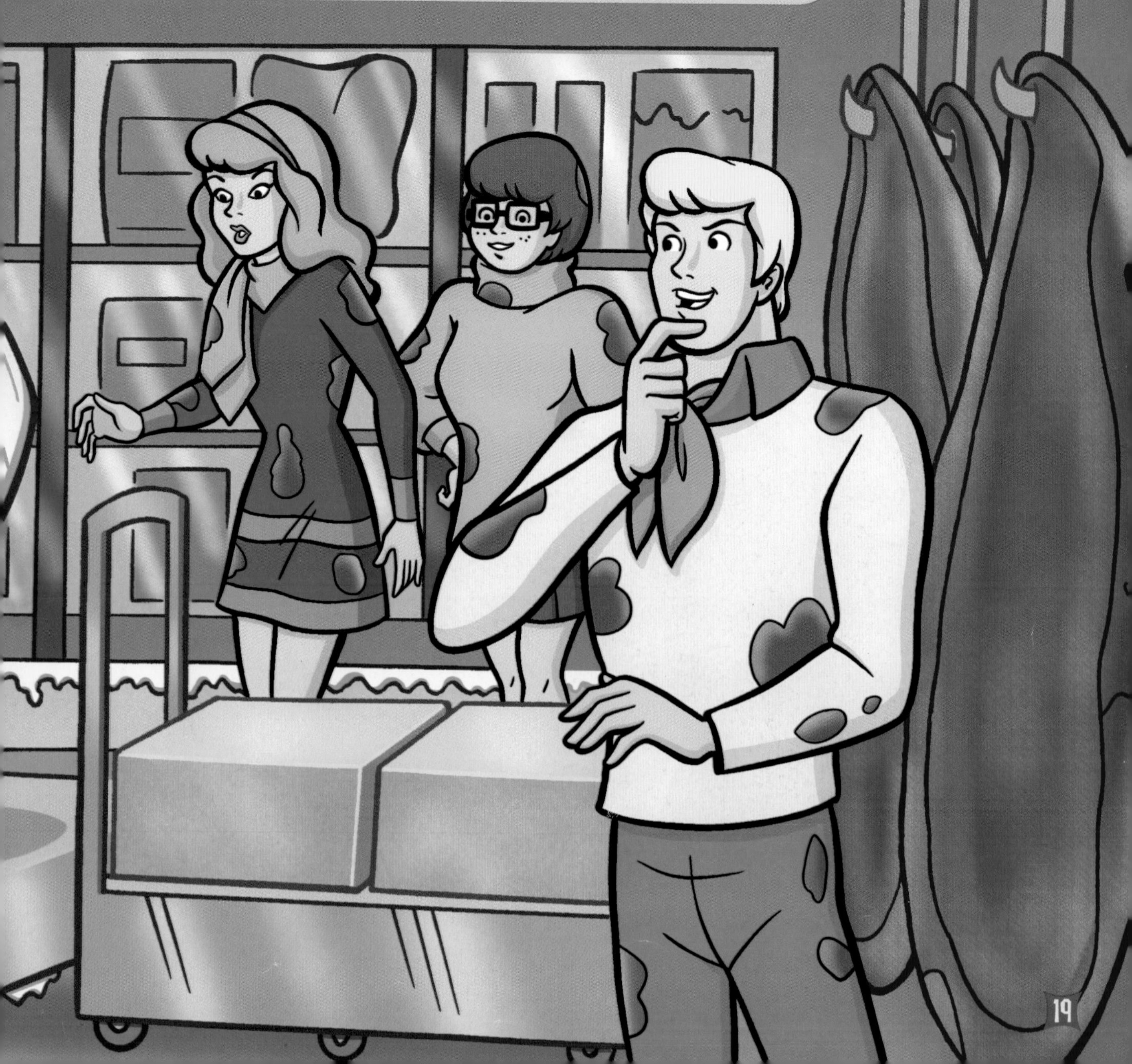

Soon, Scooby and Shaggy returned to the main kitchen—disguised as French chefs.

"Ron jour. Ron jour," said Scooby-Doo.

"Hallo. Hallo. Like, where is zee students?" Shaggy asked, with a very bad French accent. But it worked. The creepy chef appeared.

"Who have we here? Too many cooks spoil the broth, I say.

Ha-ha and tra-la-la! With my egg beater, I'll beat you away."

21

But Fred had other ideas. He pushed over a heavy ice sculpture. It fell right on top of the creepy chef! *KA-BAM!*

Then, to everyone's surprise, Mr. Kettle was pulled down from the catwalk. *THUD!*

"Jinkies!" Velma said. "The creepy chef was a puppet all along. The thin wire we found is what Mr. Kettle used to operate the puppet."

"His niece was in the cooking contest," Fred explained. "He was trying to scare all the students away so she would win the cash prize."

"It would have worked, too, if it weren't for you meddling kids and your dog," Mr. Kettle grumbled.

WELCOME CONTEST JUDGES!

Soon, the Mystery, Inc. kids were sampling all sorts of meals and goodies prepared by the students.

"This is the happiest day of my life," Shaggy cried. "How about you, Scoob?"

What could Scooby say, except, "Rooby-dooby-doo!"?